Nyra and the Lemonade Stand

by LaToya Foster

Nyra and the Lemonade Stand
Copyright © 2021 by LaToya Foster

All rights reserved. No part of this publication may be reproduced, distributed, or transmitted in any form or by any means, including photocopying, recording, or other electronic or mechanical methods, without the prior written permission of the author, except in the case of brief quotations embodied in critical reviews and certain other non-commercial uses permitted by copyright law.

tellwell

Tellwell Talent
www.tellwell.ca

ISBN
978-0-2288-5207-0 (Hardcover)
978-0-2288-5208-7 (Paperback)
978-0-2288-5887-4 (eBook)

"Nyra, where are you going?" her mom asked.

"I am going to build a lemonade stand," Nyra replied. Nyra's mom asked her if she needed any help. But Nyra shook her head and said, "No, thank you. I am a big girl; I do not need help."

"Now, how do you build a lemonade stand?" Nyra wondered. Nyra thought about all the lemonade stands she had seen.

"I know!" Nyra jumped up and said, "I need wood." So, off Nyra went to find wood.

Just then, her dad came from behind the house holding a pile of wood. Nyra ran over to her dad and asked, "Daddy, can I have that pile of wood?"

"Sure, pumpkin. What do you need the wood for?" Nyra's dad asked.

"I am going to build a lemonade stand," Nyra replied. Nyra's dad said okay and asked if she needed any help. But again, Nyra just shook her head and said, "No, thank you. I am a big girl; I do not need help."

Nyra carried the wood into the front yard and started to build her lemonade stand. But every time Nyra built her stand, it just fell back down.

"I don't get it. What am I doing wrong?" Nyra said out loud. She felt confused as to what she was doing wrong.

"You need something to hold the wood together," said Nyra's mom. "Why don't you ask your dad for help?" she asked.

"Because I can do it by myself," Nyra said.

"It is okay to ask for help when you need it. Even grownups need help sometimes," said Nyra's mom.

But Nyra just looked at her mom and said, "No, thank you. I am a big girl; I do not need help."

"Mom said I need something to hold the wood together; what could I use that holds stuff together?" thought Nyra. She walked back and forth, trying to think of what to use.

"I know!" Nyra jumped up and said, "I can use tape." So Nyra ran inside and grabbed the tape from her room.

She used the tape to build her lemonade stand and it stayed up this time. Just as Nyra was about to rejoice, a strong wind knocked her lemonade stand down.

Nyra grew frustrated again. She really thought that tape would have held her lemonade stand together.

Nyra wondered what else she could use that would hold it together. "I know!" Nyra jumped up and said, "I can use glue." Again, Nyra ran inside.

She went up to her room and grabbed her glue. "Now, I know this will work for sure," said Nyra.

Nyra carefully used the glue to stick all the wood pieces together. "Now, I just need to leave it and wait for the glue to dry," said Nyra. She didn't want her lemonade stand to fall over like the popsicle stick house she tried to build in art class without giving enough time for the glue to dry.

After the glue dried, Nyra went to look at her lemonade stand. She was happy that it was still standing and that the wind had not knocked it down.

Overcome with joy, Nyra started to do a happy dance. While dancing, Nyra bumped into the lemonade stand and the whole thing came tumbling down.

Nyra was sad. She lay in the grass and thought about her lemonade stand. No matter what she tried, nothing worked. Nyra felt like giving up. "Come on, Nyra, you can do it," Nyra thought to herself. She really did not want to give up, but she did not know how else to make the lemonade stand stay up.

Nyra told her dad about the wind knocking over her stand when she used tape and how she bumped into her stand and knocked it over when she used glue.

Nyra's dad explained that wood is awfully hard to keep together, and that is why her stand fell over when she used tape and glue.

Nyra thought about what her dad said and wondered how he was going to keep the wood together. She remembered seeing a bird house made of wood in her neighbor's back yard but she wasn't sure how her neighbor was able to keep it together.

Confused, Nyra turned to her dad and asked, "Dad, if tape and glue cannot keep my lemonade stand together, how are we going to keep it together?"

"With nails," said Nyra's dad. Nyra watched closely as her dad grabbed nails and a hammer from his tool shed. He then asked Nyra to help him by holding together the pieces of wood. As Nyra held the wood, Nyra's dad used the nails and the hammer to put her lemonade stand together. Nyra thanked her dad for his help and went to find her mom.

"Mom can you help me?" Nyra asked.

"Sure, honey. What do you need help with?" asked Nyra's mom.

"Can you help me make lemonade for my lemonade stand?" Nyra asked.

Nyra was happy to have finally made her lemonade stand. She had learned that asking for help when you need it is just as good as doing things by yourself.

CPSIA information can be obtained
at www.ICGtesting.com
Printed in the USA
BVHW021251310721
613338BV00002B/13